IT'S SHOW AND TELL,
DEXTER!

A
DEXTER T. REXTER
BOOK

LINDSAY WARD

two lions

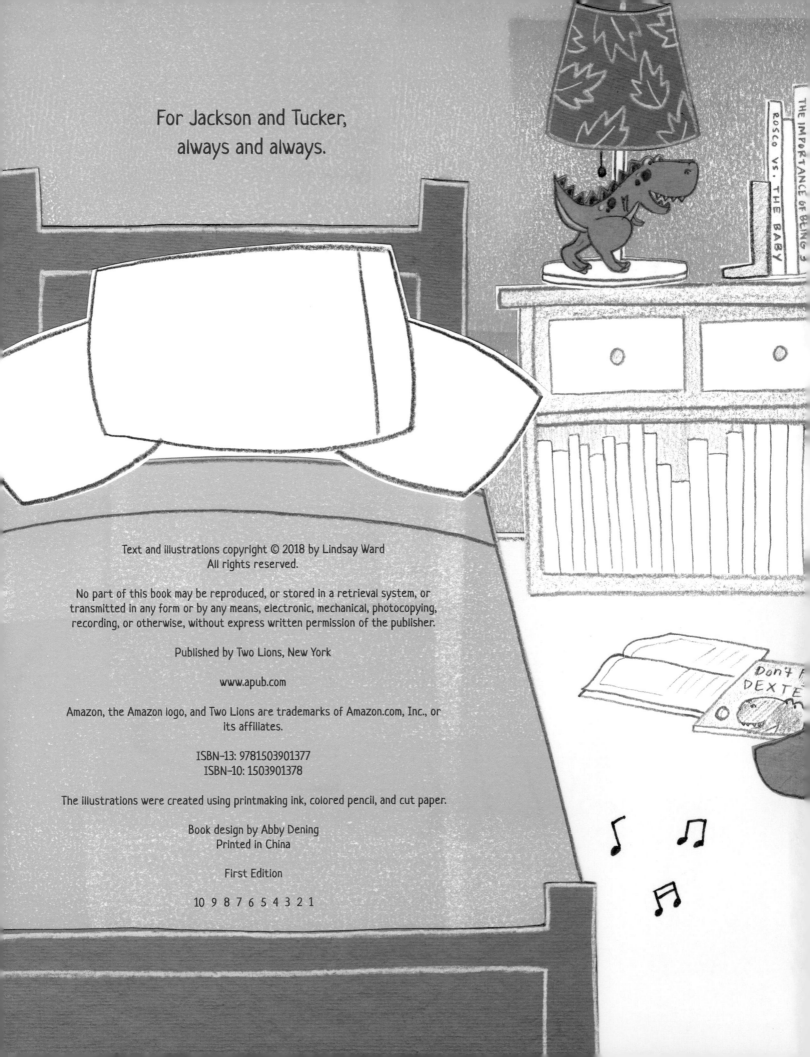

For Jackson and Tucker,
always and always.

Published by Two Lions, New York

www.apub.com

Amazon, the Amazon logo, and Two Lions are trademarks of Amazon.com, Inc., or
its affiliates.

ISBN-13: 9781503901377
ISBN-10: 1503901378

The illustrations were created using printmaking ink, colored pencil, and cut paper.

Book design by Abby Dening
Printed in China

First Edition

10 9 8 7 6 5 4 3 2 1

Oh, hi there!

It's me. Dexter T. Rexter.

Guess what tomorrow is?
I'm so excited, I can hardly wait!

It's only the most important day ever....

IT'S SHOW-
AND-TELL
DAY!

I've been training for weeks,
getting myself in peak physical condition.

5 a.m. wake-ups.

Intense workouts.

And staying hydrated.

What do you mean 'why'?

Every toy dreams of being taken
to Show and Tell.
If things go well, I'll get
super-special-keep-forever status.

Jack's been talking about it for WEEKS!
He told me he doesn't even know
what Damon and Hunter are bringing.
And they're his best friends!
(Well . . . besides me, of course.)

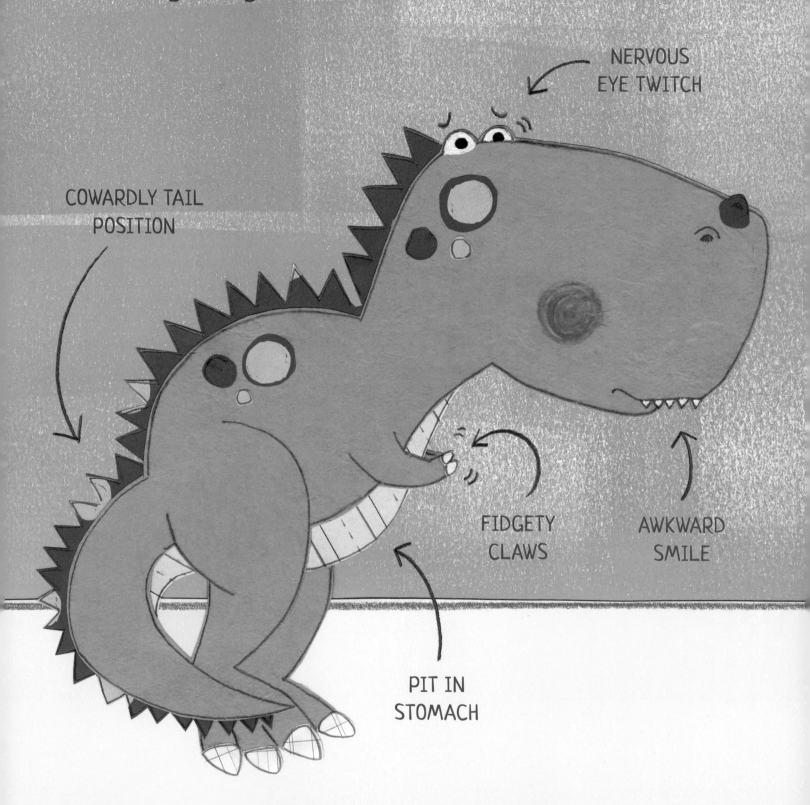

Don't tell Jack,
but I'm getting a little nervous.

NERVOUS
EYE TWITCH

COWARDLY TAIL
POSITION

FIDGETY
CLAWS

AWKWARD
SMILE

PIT IN
STOMACH

What if no one likes me?

I know! How about a costume?

That would really help me stand out.

Wait right there!

Okay, this is option number one.

Jack's class has a pet bunny.
And everyone loves it.
Jack talks about it all the time,
so I thought . . .

I know it's a little tight, but . . .

Really?

Not even the cute fluffy tail?

Sigh . . .

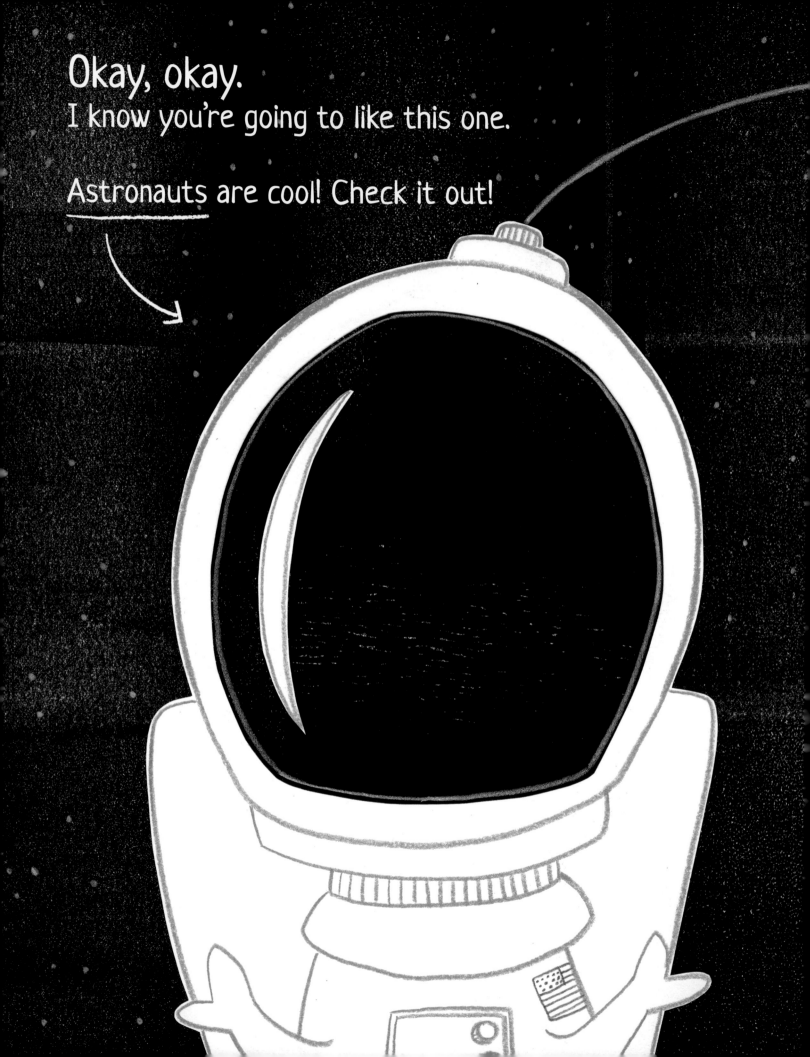

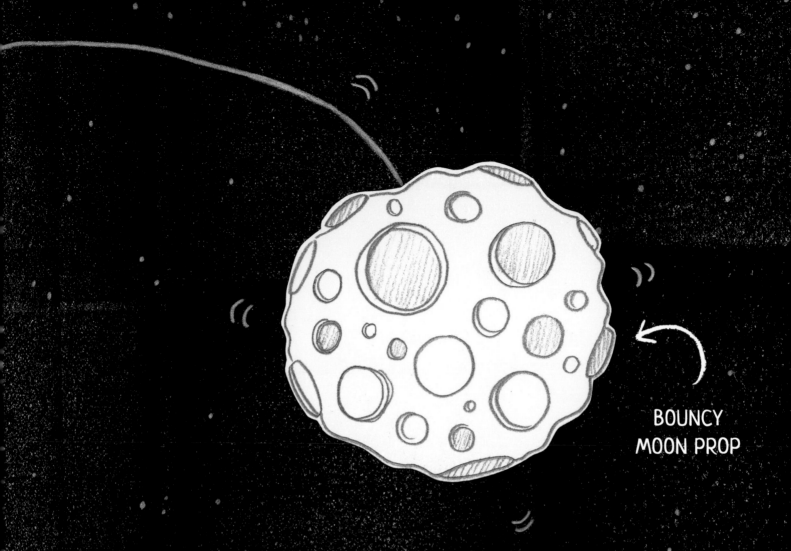

BOUNCY
MOON PROP

What do you mean you can't see my face?
I'm right here!

I see your point about the helmet.
It could be tricky.

Those were my best costumes.
And you didn't like any of them!

I know!
How about a spicy routine?

Salsa?

Mambo?

Cha-cha?

Too much?

I know! I could recite
the state capitals backward!

Uh . . . ah . . . muh . . . umm . . .

Psst . . .

. . . do you know any state capitals?
This is going to be harder than I thought.

I know! How about an impression?

Get it? It's a turtle who's fallen and can't get up.
What do you mean it just looks like a T. rex
who's fallen and can't get up?!

This is NOT good.

I don't have any skills!

I can't dance.

I can't recite!

I can't SHOW or TELL!

Oh no! What if . . .
It's too horrible.

What if Jack doesn't think I'm cool enough
for Show and Tell anymore?

He has so many toys.

What if he decides to take
someone else instead?!

1. Like Harry.

CUTE AND FLUFFY

HE HAS A CAPE!
(I DON'T HAVE
A CAPE!)

2. Or Mighty Mac.

3. Or . . . Steve.

SUPERCOOL DUMP TRUCK!

I mean, Steve's nice and all, but . . .
No, no. Jack has to take me.
I'm his favorite. He tells me so all the time.
I'm the toughest, strongest, coolest dinosaur around!
Right?

But... what am I going to do for Show and Tell?
It's going to be a disaster!

Maybe I'll be sick tomorrow?
Cough, cough.

Actually, I don't think I'll have to fake it.
My tummy doesn't feel so good.

TUMMYACHE

Show and Tell is scary.
REALLY scary.

I don't think I can do this!
I can't handle this kind of pressure!

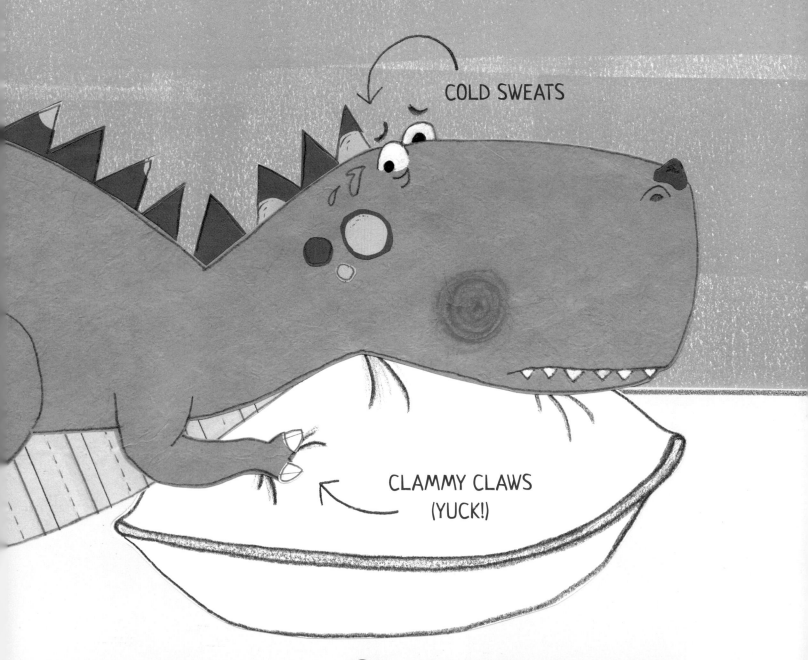

Oh no, here it comes. . . .

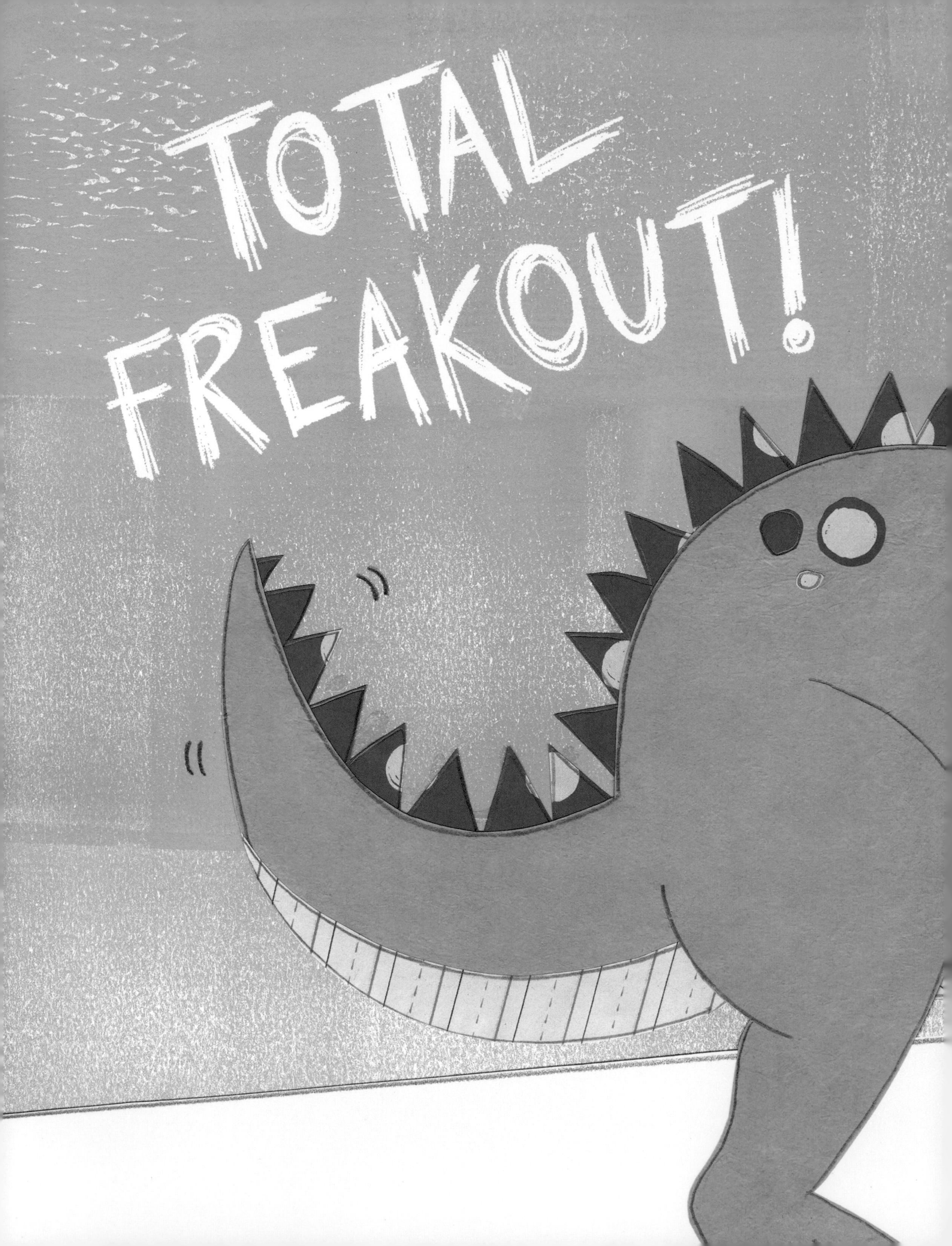
TOTAL FREAKOUT!

Deep breaths.

In and out.

In and out.

Wait,
what did you say?

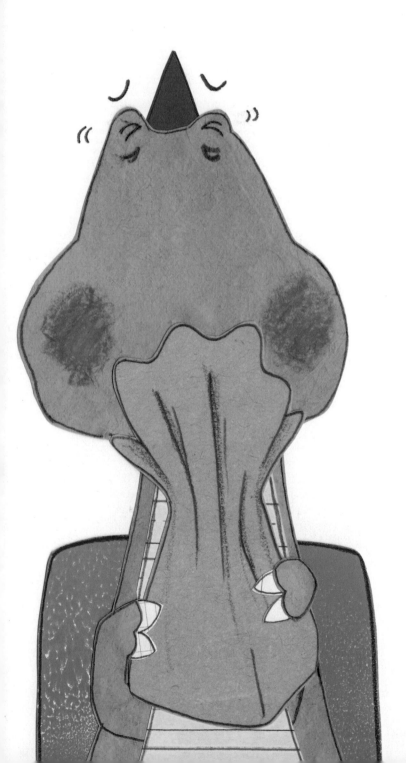

Go as myself?
That's the silliest thing I've ever heard.
I don't have a costume! I don't have a routine!
I have to have something, right?

You really think
I could just be ... me?

Hmmm ...
Well, there is one thing I'm really good at. . . .